BOUND BY BLOOD

OMAR GEARING

Wasteland Press
www.wastelandpress.net
Shelbyville, KY USA

Bound by Blood
by Omar Gearing

First Printing – February 2020
Paperback ISBN: 978-1-68111-344-9

Printed in the U.S.A.

0   1   2   3

Brotherhood, a word that has many meanings to many different people, but to me, brotherhood is loyalty, strength, integrity, and unwavering faith, even amongst your rivalry, you have your brother's back, and take solace in the fact that they have yours. This is what that word means to me, and what has been demonstrated to me by my brothers, you forever have my love, support, and most of all...loyalty.

Curtis Morris
Cameron Strickland
Jordan McClendon
Tariq Morris
Calvin James

CHAPTER ONE
Bondage

The life of a slave is very simple. Do for your master... provide for your master...live...for your master. My life was no different...being a pureblood...my fate was sealed the moment I entered this world. A prize of the Akaalian Society. There weren't many of us left...the last number I ever heard was some forty thousand....and that was fifteen years ago. Many of us who were sold throughout The Society never saw each other...we only heard rumors...whispers. I've been with my master for as long as I can remember...I don't recall ever having a family...only he. He's a very unorthodox man. Often butting heads with the elites and quarreling with other ranking members of The Akaals. They believe my people to be tools...objects to serve their purpose...then discarded...or "purified" if we are found to be defective.

Every morning...he has me fix his paste. It comes out of this bizarre contraption...hooked up to a tube that protrudes out of the ceiling. The smell is horrid...but he always finishes it so savagely...as though his life depended on it. I gagged. "Honestly... how can you down something so repugnant?" "A magician never reveals his secrets my boy..." "You're no magician...you're more of an ass clown." Eos chuckled. "I'd be mindful of that tongue if I were you, Draz." "Funny, nobody's ever complained about my tongue before, Eos." The room in which Draz and Eos were in were completely white. Devoid of color. The ceiling, the walls, everything, even the appliances and furniture were all uniform in a bland, dry white. For a man with such exquisite taste and a flare for the dramatic his big fancy house was quite...dull...at least in the eyes of Draz. Shit, it were as if they spent so much money on the rest of the house that they ran out of money to afford any paint. The interior screamed to the man's lack of imagination. Seeing Draz eyeing his household, he began to humor Draz's curiosity. "Look around you Draz, tell me, what do you see?" "A bunch of meaningless bullshit no sane man would waste his life trying to afford...why?" Eos sighed. "Cute. But besides that." "Oh, well I mean...it's hard to find something to say about the art design...or lack thereof, seeing how everything is...blank...the only words that come to my mind is...insert here." "You know, for a slave...you have a rather confined view of things." "Well forgive me, my overly dramatic master." "Where you see emptiness, I see a blank canvas, an entire world to be painted...new beginnings... new horizons...the future." "...are you high?" Eos laughed, as he walked up the stairs to his chambers. Draz walked to the giant window at the side of the room...looking at the velvety sky...illuminated by a fading sun. Draz closed his eyes...and shed a tear for his fallen brothers and sisters...no matter how far they were...he always felt them...their pain...their struggle...he could hear them...and when they were purified...this...feeling... intensified. His heart started to ache...and his mind became weak, as he felt the life drain from them. This always brought him to tears, feeling so...helpless...as his people were being hunted down...gathered, and slaughtered like animals. He could do nothing...but hope for a better tomorrow.

CHAPTER TWO
A Touch of Destiny

Draz walked downstairs to his room in the basement...it was dimly lit. His bed was rather large for a slave...his covers were made of the finest silk, and his wardrobe were filled with clothes of the finest fabrics. The room had a faint smell of incense...just enough to allow Draz to meditate peacefully. He studied the mystical arts...often spending hours of his time reading the fables and epic tales found in his master's library. Spells and charms fascinated Draz the most...though he'd never admit it, he admired his master's knowledge of magic, it were a second language to Eos, many members of the Akaalian Society look down on such barbaric practices...they see it as a mockery of the so-called "peace" they've established throughout the land.

Magic would give one too much freedom...a person who studies magic is bad enough...but if that person were to teach others...it would breed an entire rebellion. Magic puts the power in the people's hands...and they simply cannot allow that. That is partially why purebloods were prosecuted so many years ago...and why The Society is still hot on their asses now. Purebloods derive from an ancient race...the first civilization. Within them...lie the secrets to humanity...the codes to evolution...and power...power beyond anything you could ever imagine. At first..people believed the earliest civilizations to be influenced by other worldly beings...aliens. That changed when Kaz made his presence known.

Kaz was one of the first purebloods to be discovered in human history. At least the first to be recognized as...the real deal. People were skeptical...until he looked up into the sky and the clouds wept for him. Purebloods had an uncanny relationship with nature, they could speak to her...and she listened. Often times, in the old days, high ranking officials, chiefs, lords, kings...would come before these mystical beings...and they would speak to the world on their behalf. They would bless their harvest, give their wives fertility...bring rain after years of drought...there was nothing the purebloods could not do...for their bond with nature was as a mother with her child. And as a child grows to protect their mother...their home...so too, did the purebloods protect nature. Kaz stood against Themos, one of the founders of the Akaalian Society...at the time...Themos was starting the first of many campaigns which would lead to the formation of the allied nations under the Akaalian Society. Kaz knew of Themos's intent, what he sought was not knowledge or room for his people to grow and explore...but the secrets of the purebloods. He sought to ravage their land, in search of whatever it was that kept them from aging. Themos wanted nothing more than to watch his empire encompass the Earth, and he knew that the only thing that stood in the way of his selfish dreams...was time. At first, Themos offered to include the purebloods in this...new world order. But was offended by their arrogance when they so bluntly refused, humiliating him in front of his subjects. Now, he hadn't hesitated a second before swatting Kaz to the ground. Standing over him with his staff, and plunging the end into the back of his head. As the blood splattered over him, Themos felt a great amount of energy surge through him. He felt...replenished, his muscles tightened and his senses were enhanced. He could see further, hear more precisely...was this what he was looking for? He pulled the staff from Kaz's head, and rubbed the blood over his face...opening his eyes...Themos could see all. He saw the life of the world...beating...growing... and the humans dying. He could see everything connected...thriving, and he could see...at the center of it all...the purebloods. Their bodies a conduit...channeling all of nature's power...bathing in it, distributing it, it were as if they and the force of nature were one. Themos was now focused on one thing, and one thing only, the purebloods. He would live to see his empire dominate all others, he would live to conquer, to expand, to rule. And the purebloods would be the stool on which he would rest his feet. Eos was a member of Themos's bloodline, one of the most eloquent families of the Akaals, able to mesmerize and tantalize with mere words...manipulation and bribery were essential to the betterment of the human race...or so their elite society suggested.

Themos wanted to create his own race, and the essence of a pureblood was what Themos needed to do this. Draz was disgusted by this history, this process, the ordeal of his people. And as he sat there, wondering how long it would be before he were next, he heard something. It was a distinct thudding noise, coming from upstairs. He felt, entranced, as his body proceeded toward the sound. He went up the stairs...and stood in the hallway, where three doors met him. The one at the very end was his master's chambers. The door was very elegant and handsome.

And it smelled of sweet pine and fresh mint. The shiney gold handle which stood out against the ebony wood made Draz chuckle at the thought of how tacky his master was. Draz was immediately drawn to the door at the opposite end, that door. That door...the one he was told to never enter...under ANY circumstance. There were stains under the door, and the stench that came from it nearly made him vomit. The door was ugly and beaten. Mold and cobwebs covered it, and a large, menacing spider was creeping down from it's web, prancing towards Draz who, with a whisper, sent the spider marching towards his master's bedroom. Chuckling, Draz made his way into the room. Immediately, he was hit with a nauseating odor. A rancid smell so thick he could taste it. His feet squished against an unknown substance on the floor, a mixture of wet, mushy matter, whose origin Draz dreaded to discover. Draz lit a candle to get a better view of his surroundings. In the corner, quivering, was a withered, ghostly pale thing. As Draz froze, petrified by this sickening, boney figure, its head turned with a click. Its eyes were hollow and ghoulish, as if something...or someone had sucked the life out them, leaving nothing but this empty shell of a man. He were devoid of joy, devoid of freedom, devoid of light, devoid of the things that would make one human. Therefore the only thing he could be, under these circumstances...was a monster. It stood, and Draz jumped back into the disgusting puddle on the floor. The being before him was towering, its head nearly hit the ceiling, and it's face grew larger as it's body twitched to approach him. Draz cowered backward, frantically shuffling through the repulsive gooey substance on the floor to his escape, when it was upon him. The figure hovered over Draz, wheezing as it breathed it's putrid breath into his face. It spoke, "I know you, traveler." "You...know me?" "Indeed, your tale is one that brings hope to all our kind." "But...I am but a slave, what hope have I against The Society? To betray my master? How can I bring hope to my people?...I hardly even know my people." "The mind has no walls my child. Know yourself, know what is right, and you will always be free. You carry them in you, You feel their pain, their suffering, their pleas. Only the strongest of us wield such a connection to her as you do. She speaks to you when many of us rarely hear but a whisper. You are touched...my child. And now...I shall set you on your way." The creature placed its palm on Draz's chest, and a wave of immense energy came over him, his eyes closed, and when they opened..he were in his bed.

Draz felt exhausted, whether or not it was a dream, the ordeal had taken it's toll, he felt a searing pain in his chest, as he rolled over...attempting to sleep.

The pain soon subsided as he fell into a trance, reality seemed to dissipate as he lost all feeling. He were numb, and a vision had taken his senses. He were plunged in a fastly moving scene, pictures, faces, sounds, all racing by him. Strangely marked men in some...unknown land. That creature...it were guiding him...but this time it were...himself? He saw so many...so many of these men bearing these markings who were him, they were connected...HE...were connected. And then, he saw it...a box. A box bearing the same peculiar markings as those he found on those beings, and as he tried to open it, he would only find himself a few feet away from the box again, before he tried to open it again. Many times did he attempt to open it, and every time were he sent back to where he had started. This time, he sat. He sat, and began to meditate. As he felt the familiar energy of the universe flow through him...the markings on the box danced onto his skin, and they began to glow. The energy was now stronger than he had remembered, his connection was greater than it was before...he could feel...someone trying to reach him. Someone trying to tune in. As he focused...he heard a voice saying,

"Come to me..." It was hard for Draz to understand...it was too much for him to handle...that was all he could make out before he jumped out of his bed onto the floor. His head darted around the room.

He paced back and forth, pinching himself and slapping his face, trying to wake up. When he realized he was awake...he collapsed on the floor. "What the hell is happening to me..." Draz muttered to himself...he felt confused...and lost. Nothing like this had ever happened before...yet it felt so familiar...so natural. Was this what it meant to be a true pureblood? Draz's curiosity continued to peak as he noticed the box resting on his counter.

CHAPTER THREE
Awakening

Immediately, Draz leaped toward the counter, and grabbed the mysterious object.

As he laid his hands on it, his fingers began to burn, and he dropped the now glowing red cube to the floor. Examining his fingers, he noticed a strange, gooey substance excreting from his palms. A substance not much unlike that which he found in that room. At that moment, Draz almost instantly realized what this object was...a purifier.

Draz was mortified, to hold something...something so...egregious, something responsible for the deaths of so many of his kind. Something that literally sucked the life out of his people, to fuel the greed of a tyrannical aristocracy. He looked at his hands, and vomited on the floor. Draz began to wonder if this...thing, belonged to his master. And if this were his idea of some sick fucking joke. When a voice...a voice that disturbed his very being echoed into the room... "Dear me, Eos...you have an infestation." "Diamos...that is no way to address my servant, are you alright Draz?" Eos extended his hand to Draz, he raised his own, turning away from his master. "I'm fine. But are you alright...with letting this monster into our household...and why have you put THAT...that thing...into my room while I slept."

"How dare you speak to us in such a manner...you filthy creature." Diamos smacked Draz, sending his body flying through the room, hitting the wall. Eos saw his slave...his friend...hurting, in pain, but not just physically. He was hurt that the man he knew for so long...that he trusted...could be dealing with the very people that sought to exterminate his kind...that kept his people enslaved. He thought Eos was different, but now it would appear that he were mistaken.

Draz allowed himself to believe that Eos was different, that although he and The Society were of the same blood, that they were two separate entities...but as long as they provided him with his supply of pureblood essence, he would be their loyal lapdog. And now, with this box, that room, and Diamos...the head purifier of The Society, responsible for the suffering and execution of nearly half of the pureblood race...being welcomed into their...his home, as a guest. Draz knew that if he were to stay...he would be no different. It was then, when Draz's heart broke, that he felt the connection. The connection he felt in that dream. The sensation in his chest returned, and that same voice spoke to him. Telling him, "You have the key...all you have to do is walk through the door." The key...? Draz was confused...what door? Draz remembered...the cube, in his dream he could not hold it, what if it weren't the cube he were meant to access, what if it were...himself. Draz sat up. He began to meditate.

"See Eos...when you beat them, they behave...you let this beast roam about without a leash...or a cage, and it believes it owns the place. But with discipline, they all fall into line." "How barbaric..." Eos muttered to himself. Draz continued to focus...he opened himself, he let go of his master...of his feelings...of his attachment, to the man he revered. Draz found himself in a vacuum, empty of reality...or what he had believed to be...real. He had glimpses of this place throughout his life. He recalled various occasions when he would close his eyes...and he would find himself in a different world, an empty one...and every time...he would have been thinking of his people. He often found himself alone...in these thoughts...and he would cry...feeling, dreading, that one day this would be his reality...he would be the last of his kind. He almost began to cry again...until that voice...manifested into a person. "Well, hello there...Draz." The entity said. "Who are you?"

"I am...many things. I have watched as my children dwindled in number at the hands of those barbarians...and I seek to put an end to their suffering." "Where the hell are we?" "That...is a complicated question...with an even more complicated answer... you could say...in a way, this is your home. This used to be a marvelous place...a place in which your brothers and sisters would come to embrace me. I loved them dearly...that love would illuminate my entire world...but as I watched my children die... fighting to protect me...it broke my heart. And that light...died as well, and what you see now is a hollow shell of what once was. A beautiful world, a family...broken." "Why...why have you brought me here?"

"My sweet boy...I did not bring you here...you came here, you were always here...and I were always with you. As I am with all of my children. But you...you are special. I knew the moment I felt your embrace...that you would be the answer. I saw this darkness long before it came...and I knew that if I were to stop it,

I would need someone to illuminate the night...and bring their lost brothers and sisters back home. That someone...is you, Draz."

"Me...? How could I ever possibly hope to save my people? I can't even save myself." "Draz...you are...a pureblood, the powers you possess the men of this world only dream of...why do you think those fiendish ones who call themselves the elite thirst after you and your family so? Because you are their biggest threat. For so long...too long have they taken from my children.

For so long, so very long...have I awaited this day...my child. The day of your awakening. There comes a time in every pureblood's life...when they must answer a call, a call...to the forces of nature. And they are bestowed their gifts...their power...their birthright. And now...Draz, your time has come." The entity placed its hand on Draz's chest...and at that moment, Draz's eyes opened to the universe. He were...eternally... connected. Connected to a force...a force of nature. He could see all she gave birth to...the world, and the purebloods, Draz saw his people...their suffering, he saw how many there were...how many that had escaped captivity...and how many were forced to live on the run. He saw the wretched elites pursue his people...and extinguish their light. This was what caused the vacuum he were now in...so many of his people lost their connection...many of them went their lives without even forming the connection...they are lost. "I know what I must do..." Draz said "Good. Then go...go forth, and unite them. Be their guide, their liberator, their champion. You are the key to their salvation my son..." "And what shall become of you?" "My power is fading my son...I shall soon be with your ancestors...in time...I will return, when enough of your brothers and sisters are brought forth, I shall come back through your embrace. Until then...I haven't the strength to manifest myself...but, I shall not leave you...not entirely." At that moment, back in Draz's room, the cube began to glow, it was a blinding bright gold. The markings from Draz's dream appeared on the box...and like they did in his dream...they danced onto his skin, lifting him into the air, and causing his skin to glow as well. "This...is my gift to you...use it wisely my child." And with that...the entity faded. Draz mourned his fallen mother...and smiled at the hope of his people. When he awoke...he saw the slavers of the world...and sought retribution for his people...and for the betterment of mankind. "I am your slave no longer." Draz said aloud. Diamos began to laugh hysterically. "And you believe yourself to be free then?" "Free? No. I am bound by blood...but not to you." "Then what..." "A better tomorrow." And with the snap of his fingers, Eos and Diamos were cast in an ocean of blood...this was their reality...they sought what they believed gave them strength...but truly...it was what made them monsters. "Draz! Please...after everything...you would watch me die?"

"You mean as you watched so many of my kind die? No, I am not you...I simply want you to see what you are a part of...and what will become of you when we face each other again...and you are given the choice." Draz snapped his fingers again...and Eos vanished...but Diamos remained. "I do not fear death you savage!" "Good, because death is not what you face...this sea of blood is not the life-giving blood which your kind feeds on...this is the blood of the damned. And you shall spend the rest of your days among those from which you drank...as they drink from you." Withered...deformed bodies began to emerge around Diamos... hideous creatures resembling that of which was in that room. They began to surround Diamos, who started to panic. "Wait... wait! Take me back...take me! I...I can help you!" "There is nothing you can do to escape your fate." Draz raised his hand when Diamos played his final card, "I know where to find your parents!" Draz paused...then he responded, "I have already met my mother...and it is because of you that she is gone...and without you, there shall be hope of her return." Draz vanished.

"No....No!" The creatures began to swarm Diamos. "Stay back...get away you filthy parasites!" The creatures grabbed him, and began to sink their teeth into him, tearing his flesh, and feeding on his lifeforce...and just when he were about to be released...the blood would bring him back...and the creatures would begin to feed again...this would continue on for the rest of his eternity.

A fitting punishment indeed, for the head purifier of The Akaalian Society.

CHAPTER FOUR
Unchained

Draz appeared before Eos, who were now back in Draz's room. Draz looked upon Eos...with great pity, and sorrow, as he turned his back to his old, lifelong companion, and journeyed on to a new life...his destiny. And Eos shed a tear...fearing that this would be the last time they would see each other...as family.

Draz was now determined...determined to liberate his people...but to do so, he would have to find them first. So he road the winds into the clouds and meditated amongst the sun, until he felt the angst of his people. He saw so many that were lost...and found himself to be...lost. Lost as to how he...a man who were just yesterday a slave... were supposed to liberate an entire race.

Indeed these gifts that were bestowed to him were mighty...but he hadn't even fully understood them...nor did he even know what the elites were truly capable of.

That was when he felt it...that same...burning sensation in his chest. That sinking feeling...he could feel the agony of his people. So many hurting...he were determined. He rushed to the nearest concentration of pureblood activity and began to search for his lost people. He knew in the daylight he would stand out...so he raised his hand...and directed the sun to set...bringing forth a blanket of night...of which to conceal his markings. Draz strolled through the unknown territory. A ghost town...there were many of these throughout the land...areas where purebloods used to reside which were emptied whenever The Society required a fresh supply of pureblood essence. Herds of families huddled out during the busyness of day or the quiet of night to be purified...Draz's markings began to glow as visions of his people came before him. Children...infants…mothers...fathers... all collected and marched toward their slaughter like cattle. This put a strain on Draz's heart...who wept for his people...as his tears hit the ground...plants began to grow at his feet...the clouds felt his pain and frustrations...and began to weep with him.

This continued for a short while...until a strange man interrupted him. "Hello there...stranger. I don't think you're from around here." The man wielded a blade which began to steam and glow an eerie shade of blue, the blade grew brighter as he came closer to Draz...when Draz turned...he noticed that the man's eyes were different colors... the left one were a light blue with white specs around the iris...and the other were a brilliant purple with a peculiar greenish glare...like his own. "What...what are you?" The man paused... "Some call me the cure..." He drew a second blade... "But you can call me Franz..." He said, pointing the second blade at Draz. "Well...Franz...what exactly is your business here?"

Franz smirked. "Well, Draz...my business is you." Franz lunged toward Draz, slicing his torso and kicking him back. Draz flipped and slid backward...regaining his composure. He froze the rain...and sent the shards flying toward Franz, who danced around them, occasionally using either of his blades to block, or slice the projectiles. Franz's right eye lit up as he brought his blades together...which turned from a light blue to a golden yellow, and he aimed them into the clouds...which struck them...and while his blades were rich with the energy of the heavens, he hurled bolts of lightning at Draz who managed to dodge two of them...but was hit a third. He still had much to learn...now, struggling to get up...he was hit with a crippling blow...his mind began to fail him..as he could not process what had just happened...he grabbed his side as he stood on his feet, meeting his adversary...who drew ever closer to him.

"It is not your fault...your power...it is impressive..but you are simply inferior..." Franz closed his right eye...and his left eye grew bright...just like before...but the white specs...which resembled stars against a night sky...began to spin...suddenly, Draz fell to his knees. He felt weakened...then he immediately felt pain. The same pain he felt when he attempted to wield the cube. His life force was being sucked out of him. "Don't worry...I shall not drain you completely...not yet. I simply need you to be incapacitated for the trip." "Trip...?" "Yes, back to the citadel."

Franz closed his left eye...and opened his right. The green glare flashed as he opened a portal with his blade and carried Draz through it to the other side.

The desolate and quiet ghost town was traded for a bustling city-state. The change of scenery was overwhelming for Draz...whose life was spent away from the noise of the common folk. The life energy that was given off by so many of the humans there immediately began to replenish him...but he decided to mask this sudden increase in power for the moment being. The men and women of the lower level of the citadel busied themselves to and fro...most of them never even seen a pureblood before. All they know was what the upper level's inhabitants...the elites...told them. The grand lie of The Society...painting purebloods as ravenous beasts, seeking to destroy the structure and civility of their society. On this premise...Draz easily was able to walk among them...as Franz carried him to a metallic circle in the ground. Franz activated a panel...and entered in codes as the machine whirred to life. Electricity came out of the circle...and it entangled itself around both Franz and Draz...the amount of power was intoxicating...as Draz's vision began to fail him. Franz pointed his sword toward a tower far in the distance...and they shot toward the lightning rod...riding the current of electricity. They entered an insulated room with a large window facing them. Two men wearing strange suits with helmets approached them...and began to inspect Franz. They hooked Draz up to chains attached to the floor and ceiling...and exited the room with Franz. Draz could barely keep his eyes open...he drifted...swaying back and forth...until a blow to his face and gut snapped him back to his senses. A tall bearded man with a patch over his right eye stood before him. "Speak when you are spoken to...insect... and your life will be prolonged. Irritate me...or step out of line in any way...and I will gladly snap you open and have my scientists take a peak inside." The man grabbed Draz's face and turned it from side to side. "A fine specimen...yes...you will do nicely. Very nicely indeed." The man walked away toward the door, when he stopped...and turned his head. "As your new master...you would do well to learn my name. I am Themos." As Themos exited the room...Draz began to panic. "Themos...? You should be dead...you failed...how...?" Draz's thoughts were interrupted by Franz's voice...he spoke over the comm. "In a way...I suppose I should thank you. It was because of your wretched kind that Themos was able to perfect his work. Because of that first experimentation, he became the precursor to the master race, a bloodline of superior beings. I am among the first in that bloodline...the true elite. And in due time...we shall purge your disgusting filth from the face of this Earth...taking what was always rightfully ours." "You're insane..." Draz uttered. It was at that moment that Draz realized...that he didn't know who he was. He had spent his entire life only knowing what others saw him as...slave...creature...pureblood...but who was he...truly? Draz began to look inward...and he came to a simple realization. That the thing that truly kept his people in chains were not The

Akaalian Society...but ignorance...it was because of the ignorance of the people that the enslavement of the purebloods was able to occur. It was because of the ignorance of purebloods to their own people that they were unable to unite and stand against the tyranny of the elite. It was then that Draz knew what he needed to do. The markings on Draz's body began to move...and his skin glowed...his eyes opened and shone brilliantly as he broke his chains. He broke through the ceiling...and flew out of the insulated room. With the wind at his back...he rushed down to the lower level of the citadel...and put his hands against the sky...and drove the sun down to set...allowing the darkness to overtake the city-state. Up in the sky...Draz's body illuminated against the milky white moon...the people of the citadel paused...and noticed the spectacular being before them. Draz knew that his people could never truly be free unless ALL people were free. Draz decided to give the people a gift...a gift of knowledge...a gift of magic...a gift that would keep them out of the dark. He revealed to them the secrets and lies of The Society...how their success and power came...and whose backs their empire were built upon. He gave them the power of choice...to choose what they would stand for...and who they would stand by. Draz knew who he was...a man of his people...but he knew if he were to save the world...he must become a man of ALL people. As the people of the citadel marveled at this new found freedom...Draz felt an overwhelming amount of power overcome him...the people of the citadel embraced him...as their savior...their hero...their champion. They believed in him...and this belief propelled Draz forward as he rushed to liberate his people from the various purification facilities of The Akaalian Slavers.

Draz had dreamt of places like this before...they haunted his nightmares. Screams of his people echoing through his head...he had to do something. He raced toward this place...this hell. And as it came into his sight...he didn't stop...not for a second. He had burst through the side of the building...and immediately was greeted by a wave of very large, intimidating soldiers. They wore large containers filled with pureblood essence, which was connected to a tube that pumped the fluid through their veins. This supercharged them...putting them in a frenzied...primal state...these barbarians fought erratically and wildly...earning themselves the title...berserkers. As the liquid shot into their system...they each gave a bloodcurdling cry...as they rushed toward Draz...who stood strong.

His eyes gave a certain glimmer...he fought for more than just vengeance...more than just redemption...he fought for his people. And through him...their might was personified. Draz pulled the essence from their bodies...and heated their blood...boiling their flesh...reducing them to a rather large puddle. Draz shed a tear...as he felt his fallen brothers and sisters...in this fluid. He was repulsed at the fact that these...barbarians...carried his people in their veins. Draz tore down the cages in which the purebloods were huddled together..he saw the looks of awe and terror upon their face...and as he extended a hand to them...they bowed before their savior.

The purebloods embraced him...he felt the warmth of their energy and the vigor of their life-giving aura empower him...as they watched him continue on...to put an end to the tyranny of the elites once and for all.

CHAPTER FIVE
Blood Ties

The Akaalian Society were scrambling.

They were in dire need of a solution to this rising crisis...the situation was of the utmost urgency. In order to discuss a suitable course of action in response to the pureblood threat...Themos called forth the high council...which included Eos, and Demos...son of Diamos. "Brothers...I have called you before me today to discuss a most pressing matter. The pureblood known as Draz." Eos turned his head slightly...as he sweated in anticipation of the outcome of this meeting. Eos had always despised meetings such as this...but this time...it were different. It were not that he were bored, nor that he grew tired of their infernal rambling...he truly were conflicted. He did not want to lose the only man he ever grew to love...his heart ached at the very thought of this. But beyond all...Eos desired to live. His love for Draz was rivaled by his greed...for eternal life. On one hand, he wanted Draz to be free...to be happy...for them to be happy. On the other...he didn't want to give up the one thing that would guarantee his immortality...pureblood essence.

"Go ahead and spit it out..." Demos interjected abruptly. "Tell us of your little fairy tale conspiracy theories...so that this tea party may end...and I may avenge my father...and bring honor back to my family."

Themos eyed Demos... "Very well...I suspect Draz to be the pureblood of prophecy. An ancient being that I once faced long ago...it would appear that my exploits have come back to haunt me..." "And how do you suppose we go about this issue then?" Demos inquired. "Oh wait...did you not fail? Was it not you that brought this upon yourself when you tried to reason with those damn things. Was it not you...who believed that their subhuman genes held the key to some...master race? I find it hard to believe that the answer to this infestation is to mate with them. Mingling with such abhorrent blood is an abomination..." "You mean the same abhorrent blood that you shoot through your dying... insufficient veins to keep your insignificant...depleting body from shriveling like a prune and drying out in the sun...you would do well to mind your tongue child. Or I shall demonstrate what a true abomination looks like. And the answer...is simple, I have prepared for this...my sons...have prepared for this, we are ready to subdue him, and restore glory to The Society." "He killed my father..." "And your father died a coward. And you would do nothing but die or cower as he did before this ancient threat...who are YOU Demos? To challenge me...I am more of a man than your father ever was or could ever hope to be...I am more of a God...than anything your pathetic...sniveling insect of a father could've thrown his miserable life towards seeking a salvation. So you would do well...to find my favor...as I go forth to rid you of the very thing that took your daddy." At that very moment...the sons of Themos...Kiatos and Franz...entered. Kiatos's eyes were different colors...just as Franz's...and when Demos saw this..he became livid. "Filthy half-breed mutts! How dare you approach us you swine!" Themos removed the patch over his right eye...and lifting his hand...the purple glow intensified as he reached out...and forced Demos to ground...with a flick of his wrist Demos's bones cracked and his organs began to liquefy as he gave wails and shrieks of pain and pleas for mercy. Eos, looked away...horrified. Themos gave a demented smirk as he approached Demos's body. He grabbed his head, and lifted it to face his sons. "Look...upon the faces of your gods." Demos's head began to shake... "I said...LOOK!" He plunged his fist into Demos's back and gripped his spine...snapping it in half like a toothpick.

"Ahhh!" Demos began to cry. "It would appear that you seek forgiveness..." "Yes....!" Demos said in between his tears. "Well boys...you know what we do to the dogs that seek our forgiveness." "Yes, father..." Franz said...as electricity overtook his hand...he waved it through the air and it extended...a long cable of pure energy...and Franz used it to show Demos his mercy.... relentlessly…again....again....again...and again.

Kiatos looked away as Demos reached out for him to help. Eos could no longer stomach this...he began to leave when Themos caught his arm. "And where do you think you're going?" Themos asked him. "I grow tired of this...I seek the warmth of my bed." "You seek the warmth of your slave..." Eos met his gaze...then he continued on. Themos gave a crooked smile. "Run, little Eos..."

Eos found himself lost. He knew not what he were to do. Draz was all he had...how could he betray him? How...could he turn his back on his family...Eos screamed into the night. He fell to his knees...and raised his head as he heard footsteps. He recognized those echoing thuds anywhere...Themos had followed him. "We are not done yet, little Eos..." "I am!" "You are what I say you are...and you do what I say you do...your pitiful existence is so that you may serve me...little...Eos. Do not forget who made you...who gave you your eternity...I shall dismiss your insolence, for now...for I bring a gift." "What are you talking about...?" Themos held up a vial of a dark purple fluid. "Drink from me...my child...drink from me, and taste true power." Eos stared at the vial intently as the aura of the liquid enticed him. He turned away. "What do you want...Themos." "All I want...is for you to accept your place at my side. You refuse my genes...you refuse my power...at what cost? I can sense your energy, it is failing you my child. Can you not see that I fear for your future? That disgusting...vile poison that you consume is warping your mind...you are becoming attached to your food...to the enemy. They are but cattle...mindless animals that must be herded. We were dependent on them...but the master race depends on no one. We are self-sufficient...our blood is the cure to their disease upon humanity. We are the elite...because you have poisoned your system with their filth...you must purge your body of their impurity, which suppresses my superior genes...drink this, and become a god, become...the future." Eos reached out toward the vial...and Themos grabbed his hand, pulling him up, and he forced the liquid down Eos's throat. Eos fell to the ground, blood spilling out of his mouth. A disgusting, greenish-yellow moisture began to sweat out of his skin...and evaporated into the air as his flesh began to burn. His eyes began to burn as well, as his iris turned from a striking silver...to a tantalizing purple. His skin hardened, and his muscles expanded, he gave a roar into the night as Themos's genes overtook him.

Themos gave a devilish grin. "Now...let's go fetch that troublesome pet of yours..."

CHAPTER SIX
Brotherhood

Draz had liberated many of his people...and together, they went forth to free the slaves of The Society. First, they destroyed the remaining purification facilities...then, they advanced to the walls of the citadel...by this time, their numbers had tripled. Armed with the power of nature herself...the purebloods dealt the first crippling blow to The Society. Bringing down their walls and freeing the purebloods whom were being held in breeding houses. Draz watched as the people whom he blessed with their gifts bowed before him in his awesome power. A few of the purebloods looked at the humans bowing, and scoffed in disgust...as they continued on, freeing the rest of their brethren. Draz began to reach out to the people...when he heard a noise. It was a pureblood, standing before a group of purebloods, as they watched him pelting a child and her father with flaming stones. "Filthy humans..." The pureblood said, as he sent a rock headed toward the little girl's head, she closed her eyes, tears streaming down her face as she held her father's hand tightly... ready to embrace oblivion...when Draz leapt in front of them and caught the stone. Freezing it, and shattering it as he glared at the pureblood, and those who supported him. "We are NOT who they say we are!" Draz said, looking around at all the purebloods who were watching. "Let us not embody the monster they saw us as...we are meant to be better...how can you ever seek to free your brothers when you can't free yourselves of your own anger and resentment...? Chained to hatred, and revenge...bound are you...by blood, to this unruly cycle of punishment...and abuse. Look...this child...you sought her death, why? Because she resembled a people that enslaved you...yes. But you are blinded... if you were to open your heart and your mind, would you not see what I see? A people...such as you, bound to the same lawless rulers. The same cowards who fill their heads with lies and false truths. Can you not see that they are as much a slave as you?" The purebloods saw the humans...saw how they continued to bow before Draz...and how the small children looked up at them...

young minds who saw not slaves, saw not a different race...but simply...saw a people. Their people, as they approached them with curiosity and enthusiasm, rather than fear and prejudice. The purebloods lowered their arms...dropped the stones, and sank to their knees, kneeling before their wise...capable leader. A tear came down Draz's face, as he realized his people had much to learn...but his tear was not one of disappointment, But one of pride and joy, as his people embraced him as their teacher.

Draz's endearing moment was cut short...when the sun that shined down on their faces blackened as a malevolent darkness overtook them. Draz looked over his shoulder to see a shadowy figure lurking towards them. In the blink of an eye...Themos was before them. Men and women screamed as the intimidating god-like figure grabbed them, snapping their necks and discarding them as he snickered fiendishly making his way toward Draz. He pulled out a long blade infused with his raw energy and power... with a single swing he decapitated a hundred purebloods...and before their bodies could hit the ground...fiends leapt from the cloak of shadows that surrounded Themos, and fed on their corspes. Their torn, putrid flesh, which had decayed and warped due to their excessive use of pureblood essence, began to throb and glow as they devoured the precious nectar directly from the source. They were drunk with energy as they rampaged among the civilians and purebloods alike. Latching onto them and tearing their eyes and faces apart...many of them that fed too much could not store the staggering amount of power that lingered in the tissues of the purebloods, their bodies expanded as they exploded, unleashing a devastating wave of energy which evaporated anyone and anything it came into contact with. Draz stepped forward, he and his followers held up their arms as they clashed with the forces of Themos. Draz sent shards of ice, and waves of fire toward them, melting the fiends and freezing Themos's legs, the people of the citadel uplifted the earth, and sent it flying toward the behemoth they faced, they chanted as a forceful wind propelled the massive mound of earth, it knocked Themos off his feet, literally, as his body broke from his frozen feet, he fell to the ground. Draz approached him...seeing him defeated, he pointed toward his people, and the people of the citadel. "Your tyranny is at an end...we fight as one, because we are as one. And as long as there are evils such as you in this world...we will always be reminded as to why we must never forget who we are...a brotherhood...united against our adversaries...tormentors...the forces of evil. You who would mean to threaten the freedom of one..." "Threaten the freedom of all!"

The people behind Draz shouted as they came to support him. Themos chuckled. "So you believe yourself to have won? Foolish insect...this was merely the first blow." A spear landed in Draz's chest as he were pinned to the ground. Bolts of lighting rained down upon the purebloods and the people of the citadel... screaming, terror...as their bodies were fried. Franz appeared out of a portal, he dropped to the ground sending a shockwave of lightning toward a group of civilians, electrocuting them. Leaving them marred and blackened. He pulled out his blades, and began to mow down the purebloods that put up a fight. Tearing them literally...limb from limb. Draz immediately stretched out his hand...and sent his people and the people of the citadel to a faraway place...a place where they would be safe...while he fought for their freedom.

Kiatos emerged from the shadows...along with Demos, whose eyes burned red with rage as he laid them upon the very thing that took his father's life...Draz. Demos pushed Kiatos aside as he made his way towards Draz. Knocking Franz down and shoving Themos over as he began to charge Draz, taking the spear...lifting him up into the air, and plunging him down, forcing the spear deeper into his chest...Demos's hatred festered as the spear's tip began to heat, melting into Draz's flesh. Draz grunted as the molten metal seared his heart. "You will pay for what you did...creature." Draz's eyes glimmered as the spear began to freeze, Draz grabbed the spear...and broke it off, along with Demos' hands which were frozen onto it. He took the broken end and twirled it, unleashing a flurry of attacks upon Demos, his eyes shone bright as he dealt a final blow...hurling the winds of the sky toward him, sending him flying back at Franz, who grabbed him by the neck and flung him to the ground. "Fool!" Themos glared at him, "Did I not tell you...you were too weak...besides..." Themos looked toward the shadows. "...his life is not yours to take..." "Then who..." Demos said weakly. Themos smirked as Eos emerged from the shadows. His eyes...just like Draz's, glimmered as he absorbed the shadows around him...they surrounded him, empowering him...and corrupting his mind. He fed off of it...as much as it fed off of him. His eyes were a darker shade of purple than Draz's were, and when he were enchanted with this mysterious, mystical power...they had a hint of red to them...a red that threatened to consume him entirely, a red that...in that moment...blinded him to the man he had once loved. "Go...my son, go and prove yourself to me." "Yes...father..." Eos muttered as his hands were covered in blue flames. He appeared before Draz, and hit him so fast Draz hadn't even felt the blows before he were on the ground. The flames were as ice...hard and solid as they impacted his body...sending devastating chills throughout his nervous system...and as he landed on the ground...that was when he felt the burns. Long...shrieking cries of pain as he lie there in agony. He attempted to crawl away...as Eos grabbed his feet. And tossed him into the air. Eos leapt, kicking him back down into the earth, then, Eos flung himself down as well, crash landing into Draz, breaking nearly every bone in his body. Then Eos picked up his body...Draz could barely hold his head up. "Yes...now...my son, drink him...drink him and accept your place as a true elite. Take your place as a member of the master race...a god." Eos looked at Draz...and as he brought him closer so that he may drink from him, Draz placed his hand on Eos' heart. Eos' mind were flooded with visions...visions of he and Draz...together. The day he first met Draz, and took him in. The time he spent reading to Draz, and teaching him about the mystic arts. The bond he shared with his brother...the love he had for this man...a man whom he had sworn to protect...a man he would give his life for. A man he were about to kill...when Eos opened his eyes...he opened them to a kiss. A kiss from Draz.

CHAPTER SEVEN
Connected

As Draz gave him a final kiss...he fell into eternity...as his eyes that once shone brilliantly...faded...as they closed. Eos, now awakened by this kiss...his heart rekindled by the flames of his love...his love for Draz. He gasped as he watched Draz die in his hands. "Draz...oh no...no, no...Draz!" He held him into his chest. "Draz...! Don't leave me..." His eyes returned to their original silvery white as he shed a tear for his fallen love. "I know that I've caused you and your people a lifetime of hurt...all so that I could extend mine...and for that I am truly sorry..." He said as he continued to cry over Draz's body. "I've taken so much...with you I felt a little of that burden lift from me...as I grew to know you and appreciate you for who you were...and you appreciated me...you've shown me what it was like...what love...was really like..." "And I...I really love you...Draz." Eos closed his eyes as a tear landed on Draz's face. As the tear dropped...the world around Eos vanished into oblivion...as Eos awoke in an entirely different world, an empty world...a haunting blackness that crept over Eos' very soul. "What is this place..." "Our future...their future..." An entity responded eerily. "Without their liberator... their hope...darkness shall surely overtake them...and my children shall be forever lost. Chaos will overtake your world...and I will have vengeance...in my grief...as I take your world...as you have taken mine." "I want to change things..." "You cannot..." The entity enveloped him...flowing through him and over him... making him shiver, as the ghostly presence overwhelmed him. "I smell my children upon you, you are one of them are you not? But...I sense...I sense so much more inside you, not only do you consume my children...but somehow...somehow...you are..." "Yes...I am half pureblood." "Ahh...so Themos took a liking to one of my daughters..." "I would imagine so..." "And I suppose you would fancy yourself worthy then...?" "No..." "Oh...?" "No...I am not worthy...but I know who is...and I would do anything to ensure that he succeeds." Eos' heart began to shine bright...illuminating the darkness, back in the walls of the citadel, Draz's eyes gave a

slight glimmer. "I sense a great conflict in you...son of Themos."
"Conflict? No conflict...I wanted life...but without my Draz...there is no life I could have...that would be worth living." The light began to shine even brighter...as it propelled the darkness back...revealing a hidden world. A world that sheltered the people that Draz had sworn to protect. Their light began negate the dark as well. "You truly love him..." "Yes...with all of my heart...and I would gladly die for him." "Then use that...use that love...and bring back my son." Eos embraced Draz, and the markings on his body lit up, as he floated into the air. Eos' eyes returned to their purple state, as his body began to wither with old age, strands of golden yellow mist emerged from his body...enveloping Draz, filling him with power and might. His eyes opened as he felt his people bestowing upon him a gift...the same gift his friend...his love...had given him all his life. A gift Draz would use to fight the forces of evil, a gift that would unite ALL people. The gift of brotherhood. As Draz lowered...he saw Eos. And he held him...in his final moments. "My dear Eos...all your life you have protected me... you have sheltered me...you have taught me to become a man. Without you to show me what true love was...in a world so cruel to my kind...I would have never learned to love myself...let alone my people...as I now stand with

them...as I free them. Never...never could I claim to be their liberator when you...Eos...freed me." A smile came across Eos' face, along with a tear, as his eyes drifted...into infinity. A tear dropped from Draz's eyes, who was smiling as well, glad to see his master...his love...his brother...at rest. Eos' body returned to the entity, who binded his soul to Draz, so that they may forever be...connected. As Draz were connected to all purebloods, so too, was he connected to his half brother. Draz stood before the enemy, he lifted his hand, and bound them to the mother of nature, allowing her to curse them as she saw fit. Demos would suffer the same fate as Diamos, forever at the mercy of the damned, who would feed from him as he fed on so many of her children. Franz and Themos were stripped of their powers, and banished into the void...where they would spend the rest of there lives...lost... without purpose...the only thing keeping them warm, besides each other, being insanity. Kiatos was a different story...Kiatos... the youngest son of Themos...felt guilt. He were ready to face his punishment, but when he came before the mother, she saw not a criminal to be tried...but a child...a child who made a mistake. Her child, whom she must nurture, and shelter from the cruelness of the world. A child whom she must teach to do better, to be better. She decided to bestow upon Kiatos...a gift. A gift she knew one day...would free him of the shadows of his father...but to receive this gift...he must be reborn. She gave him a new name...Oriaz, and blessed his blood, so that he may be connected to something greater than himself...something that one day...he would gladly die for... A brotherhood.

THE END

Although it may be easy to lose yourself in your work...it is important to remember those who ground you, and give you purpose. Who drive you, and are the fuel of your creativity. Those that provide you the means and the resources to flourish...this is what these people are to me. Tim, and Wasteland Press, have been nothing short of a miracle for me, realizing my dream...as I hold my own book in my hands. And my mother, Mary Evans, who provides me with everything I ever needed to be successful...these are among the many things that give me an advantage, some of the reasons why I prevail, why I must prevail. To prove not only to those who did not believe...but to prove it to myself, as I am reminded by those who did.

Made in the USA
Monee, IL
13 July 2020